little Miss Tidy

by Roger Hargreaves

WORLD INTERNATIONAL

Little Miss Tidy was an extraordinarily tidy person.

In Little Miss Tidy's house everything had its place.

She had a huge handbag.

Which she would fill with all sorts of things
until she had time to put them away tidily.

Then there were all her boxes.

She had small ones,
medium-sized ones,
big ones,
enormous ones,
round ones,
and square ones.

And this was where Little Miss Tidy
tidied away all her things.

Nothing was ever left lying around in her house.

Now, with all this tidying up going on
you would think that Little Miss Tidy
was perfect, wouldn't you?

Well she isn't!

On Monday, at nine o'clock,
she telephoned Mr Clever.

"As you are so clever," she said,
"could you tell me where I put my
hairbrush when I tidied up?"

On Tuesday, at ten o'clock,
she telephoned Mr Mean.

"As you like money so much," she said,
"could you tell me where I put my
purse when I tidied up?"

On Wednesday, at eleven o'clock,
she telephoned Mr Strong.

"As you like eggs so much," she said,
"could you tell me where I put my boiled
egg when I tidied up?"

On Thursday, at twelve o'clock,
she telephoned Mr Nosey.

"As you are always poking your nose into things,"
she said, "could you tell me where I put my
serving-spoon when I tidied up?"

On Friday, she didn't telephone anybody
because she had tidied away her telephone
and she had to run all the way to
Little Miss Chatterbox's house.

"As you love using the telephone," she said,
"could you tell me where I put my telephone
when I tidied up?"

Luckily, thanks to her friends, Little Miss Tidy was able to find all the things she had lost that week.

Her hairbrush was in a glove-box.

Her purse was in a shoe-box.

Her boiled egg was in the salt pot.

Her serving-spoon was in the tool-box.

And her telephone was in her sewing-box.

Little Miss Tidy certainly was very absent minded
when it came to remembering where she
had put things when she was tidying up.

But she couldn't help it.

On Saturday, it was her birthday and
Little Miss Chatterbox came to her house,
carrying a splendid-looking parcel all tied
up with red ribbon.

Little Miss Tidy couldn't wait to see what
was inside the present.

It was a notebook and pencil.

The perfect present for somebody who lost
things as easily as Little Miss Tidy.

Little Miss Tidy was as happy as ...
well, as happy as Mr Happy.

She spent the rest of the day opening all her
boxes and writing down in her notebook
everything that she had stored away in them.

It was very late by the time she finished
her list.

She went to bed, very tired.

On Sunday morning, she woke with a start.

"My notebook and pencil!" she cried.

"Where ever did I put them when I tidied up?"

Little Miss Tidy spent all day Sunday
looking for her notebook and pencil.

She had to open and close all her boxes again.

And do you know where she eventually found her
notebook and pencil?

... on her bedside table!

MORE SPECIAL OFFERS
FOR MR MEN AND LITTLE MISS READERS

In every Mr Men and Little Miss book like this one, <u>and now</u> in the Mr Men sticker and activity books, you will find a special token. Collect six tokens and we will send you a gift of your choice
Choose either a <u>Mr Men</u> <u>or</u> <u>Little Miss</u> poster, **or** a Mr Men or Little Miss **double sided** full colour bedroom door hanger.

Return this page **with six tokens per gift required** to:

Marketing Dept., MM / LM, World International Ltd., PO Box 7, Manchester, M19 2HD

Your name:_____ Age: _____

Address: _____

_____

_____Postcode: _____

Parent / Guardian Name (Please Print)_____

|← 100 mm →|

ENTRANCE FEE **3 SAUSAGES**

MR. GREEDY

25±0 mm

Please tape a 20p coin to your request to cover part post and package cost

I enclose <u>six</u> tokens per gift, and 20p please send me:-

<u>Posters:-</u>   Mr Men Poster ☐   Little Miss Poster ☐

<u>Door Hangers</u> - Mr Nosey / Muddle ☐   Mr Greedy / Lazy ☐

Mr Tickle / Grumpy ☐   Mr Slow / Busy ☐

20p   Mr Messy / Quiet ☐   Mr Perfect / Forgetful ☐

L Miss Fun / Late ☐   L Miss Helpful / Tidy ☐

L Miss Busy / Brainy ☐   L Miss Star / Fun ☐

Stick 20p here please

Please Tick Appropriate Box

We may occasionally wish to advise you of other Mr Men gifts.
If you would rather we didn't please tick this box ☐

Collect six of these tokens
You will find one inside every
Mr Men and Little Miss book
which has this special offer.

1 TOKEN

Offer open to residents of UK, Channel Isles and Ireland only

Mr Men and Little Miss Library Presentation Boxes

In response to the many thousands of requests for the above, we are delighted to advise that these are now available direct from ourselves,
for only **£4.99** (inc VAT) plus 50p p&p.
The full colour boxes accommodate each complete library. They have an integral carrying handle as well as a neat stay closed fastener.
Please do not send cash in the post. Cheques should be made payable to **World International Ltd. for the sum of £5.49** (inc p&p) per box.

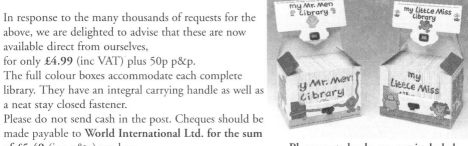

Please note books are not included.

Please return this page with your cheque, stating below which presentation box you would like, to:-
Mr Men Office, World International
PO Box 7, Manchester, M19 2HD

Your name:_____

Address: _____

_____

_____Postcode: _____

Name of Parent/Guardian (please print):_____

Signature:_____

I enclose a cheque for £_____ made payable to World International Ltd.,

Please send me a Mr Men Presentation Box ☐

Little Miss Presentation Box ☐   (please tick or write in quantity) and allow 28 days for delivery

Thank you

Offer applies to UK, Eire & Channel Isles only